NO. 9
WINTER 2026
ANNIVERSARY EDITION

MIDSUMMER DREAM HOUSE LITERARY & ARTS MAGAZINE

CALIFORNIA

Midsummer Dream House
San Diego, California
United States

Paperback ISBN: 979-8-9993991-7-5
Print ISSN: 3064-7819
Printed in the United States

midsummer dream house

LATHER

CONTENTS

POETRY

MEMOIRS

FICTION

ART

WHAT IF THAT'S ALL IT IS

What if it's all a weird sugar rush induced dream, and I'm actually on my desk in second grade covered in glitter and about 5 minutes away from forgetting what this was all about..

MEANDER

My nails meander places searching for fervor. Past thighs, Down legs, in soft spaces. Searching as I lean in for a kiss to fuel the frolic. A moan escapes before mine as to furnish another future. It will be bodies pressed to passion as we intertwine every circumstance.

NIBBLE

I run my nails across the belly curiously wondering if needs are being met. In the quietness I attempt to connect more deeply to the necessity. Have I fed enough love to nibble the fleas of discontent away? Are my teeth more loving than history? Has the past been forgotten?

INK

Ink your breakable lines across my heart. Urge is just an ignition jump start to my ocean of love. I want to open my subtle floodgate. I thirst for a love unshielded in a waterfall of trust like we're young again. I've grown weary of the walls I've constructed like memorials.

AWAKE

I awake with dreams of you flashing through my hair. Streaming the greatest one's, I smile in hopes for a new daylight. I marvel at the sheen of a rejoicing smile that's been given by this life. It fits so nicely in the caring.

POLLEN

If pollen could open eyes would we be rolling in flowers for vision? Would we crush another beautiful part just to be bathed in wisdom? I say leave the loveliest of things to be taken in without plucking its power to experience another's life as a gift given.

LAURA SUTHERLAND

GOATS TEACH ME THE MEANING OF IT ALL

I hear tomorrow
there is to be snow,
but I sit now in the grassy pasture
with the goats, reading poems to them
Oh what a treat! They nibble
at the pages until they realize
it's not actually quite so nice;
words filling my heart
are merely an unsatisfying snack
They play in the warm sun
Bringer of both life and death, simultaneously
but in this moment it is simply
the harbinger of a joyful life

RAINA GAVIN

SEA GLASS

I could be happy here with him. In the land of dim, warm milk.
In the embrace of our sun-lit den. In the consistent creaks
of our box-spring bed. We are so careful in our quiet world
not to rouse the dead, not to shake away the perfectly dosed
fine dust of sleep flaked across our waking eyes.

A temptation, always to empty my head and rest against
his solid chest; a most familiar perch. I am back out
of myself, swallowing down, again, the lurking truth.
It's come clear this year – This creeping, glossy, Gothic
Spring, where flowers bloom with impending doom -

I don't know what it is that I want, or if it is him,
or how long he'll wait as I chip at the paint
of our shining veneer. I am digging deep into my own
great mystery and praying that I uncover some evidence
of permanence. My fingers can't stop feeling for damage.

We're back at that old impasse.
Escape routes shine like sea glass.

THOMAS DIMASSIMO

THE UNIVERSE OVER

In the next universe over, you still have my hoodie, because we're still together. Once again, we're sitting in that diner watching Khalil's world crumble after he foolishly orders the disco fries. Our bellies hurt from laughing, but nothing else does. Below the table you stroke my palm with your thumb, and I never let go. We don't know why we're so lucky in the universe over, but it's only because of our failings here. It's okay. We had to learn so they could grow. We exhausted our hearts, so in the universe over, theirs would be made big enough to last.

DAMON HUBBS

NINE LINES & ONE FROM GERTRUDE STEIN

look at the view from the carriage window
the sea's wet mouth venturing into tastelessness
a sinuous, far off voice   lascivious as oyster flesh
the sun's orphic gleam daring you to start your own line of sunglasses
that summer we ate every oyster in Brittany
your mouth brined with mine   loud, willowy
we talked of suicide & oranges
unmoored between the major & minor there is everything
and, then there is everything else
i called you Marie & we were as spoiled as the world

ANDI LEIGH

MOONLIT MEMOIRS

Birdsong in
The red warm sky,
Toasting the air
Before night veils.
And crickets hum
Orchestrating,
Within swaying cattails.
Lightning bugs
Mirror the stars,
While birdsong
Fades to stillness
In moonlit memoirs.

First published in *Burn the Felt Heart*

JAY GOLDIN

EMBRACE

a little while
a little world
of our own

For C.S.

NEIL G

UNTITLED

chance meeting with a tiny stream
so here I'll sit, and here I'll dream

JUNAID AHMED AHANGAR

A FAILED POEM WITH NO METAPHORS

I'm writing a poem for you with no metaphors.
I've failed before.
I'm distracted by my second hand heartache.
I've tried changing rooms, shifting houses.
It's still the same.
I want to write a poem for you with no metaphors.
I'm failing already.
I'm distracted by your souvenirs.
Am I holding this photograph or am I holding your hand which shivers just before you click?
Let me scratch and claw my way into your gypsy knees and cry in your lap.
I am in the middle of writing a poem for you with no metaphors.
Stepping back is hard.
Convincing myself is difficult.
Walking away is my own civil war.
You're just out of reach, you're just out of reach.
This poem is going nowhere, I have no metaphors to hide behind.
Your aching hand looks like a sick heart.
It's all been said before, borrowed words.
How do I tell you in words never spoken before in this world?
The dismal failure of my longing.
Will my words carry more weight if I send them to you in a letter? I must.
This is not a poem.
These are the incoherent ramblings of an old man who tried.
Only to realise that it was all mere consolation.
The sun does not go down the same for you.
We do not live under the same sky.
I forget a lot these days, turning off the stove, suits, places, people.
I forget about forgetting you these days.
I forget why I'm here, the end of a poem filled with metaphors.

THE DEVIL'S BRIDGE

no matter where i be   i do look down to the hands
  see them covered in our tacky peat

here people ask   *are you a garden-er?*
  of sorts   i say   as if i can get close to it

and even here by the lakes   i can't wash them
off   a man in the continual act of burial

and the hills and the bridges and people try
to stop me   all the scrubbing   editing

takes you further from cleanliness   all my moments
  tied into the filth of this old fuel

once a last chance income for the lost medievaller
  i am the lindow man himself   you know?   it is me

always a leathered heart creaking for lost beats
  always some kind of turbid memory to search for

sometimes preservation is progress   sometimes
  i pull oak from the ground in wilmslow   and i

pray with it over the river lune
  as if a trip up the M6 means salvation   redemption

BRANDON T BENNETT

MORNING IN A CITY

a cross hangs from the wall   the fall of winter
is heavy on old panes and the thin arms
of my pale friend droop like weeds
over snow covered hills   the soft canter
of her blood pumping on my ribs   still
i cannot reach her at this time

we could be a hopper   i'm sure
you've seen the one
a train pulls out the station below
   it cuts through the drumming
maybe we will grow old   maybe
there will be a rome for us   and maybe

i will learn to separate my stomach
   this soul   from shadows of dionysus
like a salmon's final swim   these moments
were born to be forgotten   or consumed
if i try hard enough i know what it is
to be the rain   landing on tired hotels

UNTITLED

I wish one of us
would get too drunk and call
a hundred times, but
we're both too sober and
no one's calling at all

TESSA YOUNG

THE WHIRLWIND NIGHT

Soft changing Lights projecting Against naked bodies Playing hide & seek With the foregone. Aftermath of forsaken Goodbyes & parted Pages torn from Books never closed (Books never opened).   In the heart of hearts- Cold smile shatters- Yet daffodils blooms Under snow- These hollow lot Hallways echo In chamber Grievances: "You were My home" – Curtains drawn low- No sunlight to be Let in (& never to be Ushered in By your Skeleton hands)

DONOVAN BALDWIN

UNTITLED POEMS

i turned and reached out
one last blind attempt at love
groping for your hand

***

anchored by the earth
mountain tree plain or ocean...
i am most free

***

dawn finds ecstasies
making love to you in dreams...
ending with sad sighs

***

single wisp of cloud
drapes moon in brief negligee
baring silver skin

***

each morning dreams end
all memories fade away
i cease to exist

SHAYNE JOHNSON

RECHER - ITALIAN ARCHITECT

5.28.15

On Tuesday morning after spending too much time awake the night before, I get this odd WeChat from a coworker that asks:

“can you do me a favor? My friend need a foreigner to attend a meeting as a architect to henan province from this afternoon to tomorrow afternoon. they can pay you 2000-3000RMB, it is a emergency. In addition, they can pay you all the fee for train and hotel. would you want to do this?”

Of course my first thought is:

“chyeahh getting paid to travel!”

.. followed by ..

“$400-$500 dollars!”

.. followed by ..

“is this a different form of prostitution that I’m unaware of?”

Taking my chances I agree to this meeting and begin my long 30 hour journey to Puyang, a small city near Hebi. Puyang has about 1 million people, but you don’t see them. Or maybe this is my constant surrounding of 24 million people that makes 1 million seem empty.

Whatever the reason, Puyang is growing..and fast. A city of infrastructure and development as well as growth and promise. Skyscrapers being built by the dozens EVERYWHERE! But no one around to live in them..

Nearby rivers were rerouted so that lakes could be formed with beautiful plateaus of concrete surrounding the shores.

All be it with no one to enjoy it...yet.

However, none of this is clear upon my arrival, it will take a whole day for me to see this and ask questions to myself.

—

My journey starts via subway where I meet Mona, an architect from DaQing (near Harbin) who works for this architecture firm. We subway to train, then bullet train to Hebi. From Hebi we have a driver take us 50 minutes East until we reach Puyang.

Hungry and tired, yet still eager to explore, the driver takes the 3 of us to a nearby restaurant. All traditional Chinese food and enough food to feed a family of 12. My Chinese is still pretty low at this point and communication to everyone is at a minimum. My lack of verbal skills are made up by me eating, and eating, and eating.

It seemed like the only thing I could do! It was awkward, however, that's soon interrupted by a full glass of beer. Then another, and another... and another.... And so on.

The driver… THE DRIVER is cheers-ing me every 2 minutes. He orders more beer, more food, then invites a lady friend who ends up spending the next 24 hours with us at meetings (little to my knowledge).

Man, by midnight, I was more than a bit tipsy and had to be up at 6:30am to meet with the people who thought I was somebody else.

Turns out, a Western Face is needed to appear at meetings all day. The original guy couldn't make it because of food poisoning.. but I know better… come on guy.. you don't want to travel all that way to a weird city for no extra pay to listen to people speak a language you don't know ALL day just to turn around and go back home.

So, this is where I step in:

SHAYNE JOHNSON

I'm Recher, a 30 something year old Italian Architect who lives in Beijing. Not just an architect though… I'm Chief of Outlets.

Turns out, Recher is the Chief Architect of a chain of Outlet stores across China… Dozens from what I took away in the mess of Chinese PowerPoints that I sat in.

My day starts:

07:00 – 07:30 Meet Mrs. Wang (who speaks little English and says one thing with a smile: "You…… um…… don't say anything.")

HaHa!!

07:30 – 08:00 Find where we're supposed to be for breakfast.

08:00 – 09:00 Eat and Greet with 20 people for a traditional Chinese Breakfast.

This is insane.. I can't even begin to explain the thoughts that enter, leave, and re-enter my brain for the next 60 minutes. Of the 20 or so people, seated strategically around a large circular rotating table, I know 2 of them. And my knowledge that extends beyond this is:

1. don't speak at all.

2. pretend you're the Chief Architect (knowledge passed through a whisper at the breakfast table from Mona, "Psst.. Sh'en… You are Recher. You are Chief Outlet Stores.")

I reverse around the clockwise rotating table to my seat which, why the fuck not, is right next to the most important person in the room.. Mayor/President of Puyang. On her other side is the boss of "my" architect firm.

Words are spoken, eyes haven't left my direction in about 3 minutes now, and I start to blush as some "hellos" are thrown my way with occasional head nods and smiles.

I don't know where to look so every time someone looks my way I instantly begin eating. I go through 3 bowls of soup before making eye contact with anyone. My broken understanding of Chinese has left me impaired against the "lao wai" remarks.

By the end of breakfast, I find myself escorted out in front of many women and pushed next to the VP.

My next adventure begins in an oversized conference room. Soft, sponge-like carpet allows me to walk as if I'm on the moon to my oversized Chair. I'm serious, these things were built for emperors and kings, not for the likes of my inadequate skyscraper abilities.

And where does this chair sit? Second in line to the boss of my company who is having a press conference with the President of Puyang. The numbers in the room have doubled – 40, maybe even 50 people are present as I sit… only white guy around, listening to the "SNAP, SNAP" of cameras and the shuffling of the reporters' feet.

Unaware that the President has walked in, I am sitting way too casually at this point to get up and shake his hand. He walks to me, I quietly say, "Shayne, nice to meet you" before realizing I'm not Shayne…

-shit-

I resume my position and the next hour is consumed by another language driven partnership that I cannot
comprehend. Around me is an additional row of gigantic chairs that are filled with Chinese Government
Employees. Top of the Rank for this growing city.

Dismissal is called. Another round of handshakes completes another step in my day as Recher: Italian Architect.

———

SHAYNE JOHNSON

I can't help but imagining myself as George Castanza, or rather, Art Vandalay of Vandaly Industries.

———

I'm guided along the corridors with the ranking officials to another room where 90 minutes of PowerPoints in Chinese are presented.

Never in my life had I been so bored. I literally had to pinch my inner thigh every 30 seconds to make sure my heart rate stayed above 10 beats a minute.

I try to look at the men in charge with an authoritative "I Know" face.

Did I mention that this time, I was sat directly across the table from the guy giving the presentation on his city, and right next to "my" boss giving a presentation on MY building??

Presentation concludes..

Another round of food.. same seating position, different room… even more different food. Instead of cutting meat up for us, it looked as if the chef found a baby lamb – made it bite on a piece of its own bone, then threw it in the oven.

I swear, this thing was the ugliest, most terrifying thing I'd ever eaten. The Government Official in charge at the table, seated on my right arm, looks at me, cheers only mine and his glass, and then stands up to make a toast. This goes on 15-20 more times??? At least until he uses his own chopsticks to pull out the "best part" of the meat to give to me. I was stuck, couldn't say no now… (actually I wasn't supposed to say anything) so I took it half-eagerly with a "Xie Xie."

The mutton was better than it looked, I'll give it that.

A few glasses of wine, some funny things said back and forth and a semi-full tummy, our lunch ends. As short as my description might be, this was as equal, if not more awkward than breakfast. All these people at the table with the highest ranking people in the city. They burped more than they talked and slurped their soup worse than a man with no arms. Table manners that I grew up with didn't exist in this new world.And then, the field trip begins:

First we go to the Urban Planning Center and get a full tour of what this city plans to be in the very near future. Incredible. Skyscrapers, Lakes, Public Buildings and a full scale city able to withhold so, SO many more people.

Next, we all walk out of the hotel dining area and down 4 flights of stairs. We all gather into a huge van for 15 and two cars follow us. We're led through the entire half-built city, stopping at future locations of boardwalks and restaurants, hotels and bars, malls and shopping centers. All with foundations and pillars, but completely empty and see-through.

We stop on a bridge dubbed "The Music Bridge" with musical notes molded into the metal railing across the walkways. I guess music will be played here when the city decides to "open up."

Then, to my surprise we stop at my build site of this Outlet Mall that I'm responsible for. It's hot out, I'm so tired at this point, but the thrill of being someone I'm not is starting to get to me.

Everywhere I go there's people taking pictures of me. Not a single photo was taken without somebody read justing their position so that I could be in the background. It was hilarious.

And so, we pack things up and begin the long journey home.

I wait in the hotel for too many hours, catch up on a few episodes of "Curb Your Enthusiasm," then take the bullet train back to Beijing. I make it home by 10pm the next day and negotiate my way to 250.

SLEEP

Morning light invades the dark room. I try to pull the curtains tighter, but they come undone.

I want to sleep. Not a washing machine type of sleep that mixes dreams and problems. Fights with
fathers threatening disownment (get a real job, senseless dreamer), juggling manuscripts with ease, while
deadlines hum impatience.

The sun bursts even more across sheets, stained with history and sweat.

I can't sleep on that.

I pull on sweats, grab my computer. Head out the door. A breath of morning air greets me. I don't know where I'm going, but I'm going. It's a small relief.

EARLY SPRING

Phil predicts an early spring. They tell me it's a foolish ritual; a rodent can't predict the weather. But who can? I didn't know I'd move from one apartment to the next, leaving behind puke-green TV dinners bought on tenuous credit and people telling me to pick myself up by the bootstraps, while bosses talked about streamlining, budgets, fake regret.

I look out the window. Snow still covers the ground, tree branches naked and tender. But there's a patch or two of brown. And the moon escapes a cloud, shadows waltzing into my new room. Perhaps the ice will break completely.

ALEXANDRA

I just want to tell you I'm sorry.

The minute the boat left for the sea, I threw a bottle into the water and watched it ebb to the shallow part of the bay only to surf there among the foam spots.

I'm sorry this voyage isn't going to end any time soon. Strange. This tipping and riddling of water with no land in sight. Only God's out here, teasing you with his requiems of silence.

Can you practice your dancing for me despite my absence? Captains need to know their daughters are safe and happy and dancing. Captains can't steer their ships if their children are drooping their heads and crying.

I'm sorry that you broke your ankle when running to go play with the other children. How acutely I remember your cries. Carrying you home through trees and brambles with thick raindrops beginning to fall. Your wailing when the bone was set. Your wishing that Mother was by your side, the delirium of your pain recasting her image before your eyes, setting itself next to me, tricking you with smiles and calm hands.

Out here, it's unclear what we're looking for. The pirates, former citizens gone bad, who have harmed and plundered our people, yes, but where are they? They are ghosts in the mist, shadows of Leviathan that taunt with the tips of their vessels and then vanish. Every sailor looks beyond the confines of his original mission and hopes to find more—to chance upon another world. We cannot even find what we're supposed to be looking for.

Rubies, emeralds, and gold bars, form the curvature of the earth and ridicule my view of what really matters. You!

Every man over the history of the world has sought the mystery beyond the horizon while forgetting to tread his own waters first. Till your soil and unearth the gems therein. Toss your ambitions to the winds! Turn your eyes to the trees in your midst. Stop trying to build wings to observe and control the forest.

If it were only that simple. This new world we're living in is simplicity subverted, dear one—an innocent hand pricked with brambles and left to bleed.

If we don't go, they strike at night. If we don't pursue them, they will pursue you. If we don't sink their ships, they'll sink ours.

You once asked what the hardest part of a voyage is. I say it's the lone liness. We are a month into the quest and the ship has become the sole organism and the sailors are its trembling parts, the limbs sharing in the same desolation. Pretty soon the creaks of her great sides indicate our longings for a harbor. The whining of a mast in the wind is the creaking of my heart. We are alone, alone together, until the ship signifies the whole world, spinning through the waters of the cosmos.

I'm sorry we have not found and killed the pirates yet. They set a strange course. They melt into islands and become waves. They slip past us in the dead of night. They are the shape shifters, darts carving wounds in an ocean designed for happier ventures.

Sometimes it pains me to the point of wakefulness that I've left you with your uncle, who is a good man, but have nevertheless left you for a quest whose object feels so evasive. Days pass without even a hint of these macabre men. The other day we had a bout of doldrums. The ship stayed in one place for a week. The men sunned themselves on the deck. We fixed everything that needed fixing. The top of the foremast. The splintered decks near the cabin. The arm of the Madonna reaching out to the great nothingness. I joined my midshipmen at the helm and explored the crystal horizon through eyeglasses. An albatross wheeled and glided a mile away. It burned white, cross-like, and then vanished.

But enough about me. Enough about this voyage. How are you, daughter?

Have you planted the strawberries on the plot of soil your uncle gave you? He was kind to let you have your own section of the land. What all will you do with the strawberries? Will you mash them to make a jam? Will you juggle them in your hands and then feed them to the deer that move slowly through the forest?

I'm sorry that such questions will never reach you. We are so far from any port city. I'm sorry that the only person I'm writing to at the moment is myself. Madness is aloneness turned in on itself. And it's worrying that the pirates have drawn us out only to skirt us and attack you while our best men are at sea, chasing ghosts and dreamless horizons.

I'm sorry, Alexandra. We're lost, lost, lost. Another bottle into the sea, with no message inside. No message will do except our ship itself announcing itself in your line of vision. I want to see you running on the edges of cliffs with no fear of falling. I want to catch you if you were to fall. That's all I ever wanted.

With a storm ahead, and monsters swimming beneath me, I fear this is a eulogy, self-written, gone to be unread as you plant your strawberries so far away. Just plant them deep, water them when it doesn't rain, and wait for me.

PETER BILES

THE FISHER'S MAN

At first it was just the fisherman on the river, up to his waist in the water. He sent long casts out into the current with his fishing pole and slowly reeled back his catch. I was standing on a knoll farther upstream but could see him well. I could see his green waders, his broad-brimmed straw hat, and the cigarette in his mouth producing a thin trail of smoke. The water was dark. You could see nothing beneath its surface. All you could see were the ripples caused by the little worm at the end of the fisherman's line, and the evening sun laying golden fingers on the far bank.

I did not know where I was. I stooped to touch the water at the base of my feet. It was not as cold as I might have expected. And it sort of clung to my hand when I drew it out, like it was asking me to stay. The air was silent. All silent, except for the fisherman's bait making soft plops in that slow, deep, broad current of the river.

Something told me I knew this man who fished so ardently. Had I seen him somewhere before? Was he an old visitor in my dreams come to haunt me one more time? I didn't know. There was no telling. All I knew was that I saw him raising his big arms overhead to cast, time and time again.

He brought in a fish. It was a trout, violent red. He tucked it in a basket by his side. At the next cast, he brought in a golden bass. Next, a small marlin. And finally some grubby catfish, a wriggling green eel, a cantankerous gar.

He caught each one without upset. He tucked them all in the basket like they were books being put on a long shelf.

How many fish he caught I will never know. It must have amounted to more than fifty. For a long time, he caught nothing. But he never altered the rhythm of casting and reeling. Not once did he take a break. Not once did he raise his shadowed face to look at me standing there overhead, trying to articulate the frontier before me.

Beyond the river there was a wall of pine and spruce. The front trees were ignited by the twilight. The spaces between the trees made columns of golden light, but exposed no living thing in their ranks. The rest of the forest was dark. A mystery. I wanted to throw a stone into the river to see what kind of sound it might make. I wanted to swim in the river, but felt like this was not a river for throwing stones into or for swimming in. One needed green waders and a broad-brimmed straw hat to get into the river.

As I was looking across the water, a figure appeared on the opposite bank, right across from the fisherman. I could not see his face, but he wore a gray trench coat with a gray hood over his head. I had no idea where he had come from. The only explanation is that he just stepped out of the trees. There was no other place he could have been hiding. But he took out his own fishing pole, and after tying a silver hook to the end of the translucent line, made casts into the river. He made long casts, so long that the hook fell right next to the fisherman. I mean right next to him. The man on the other side of the river would raise his pole over one shoulder and loft his missile with perfect precision. But the fisherman did not seem to notice the hook. Maybe he did not want to notice. He kept up his own fishing. He drew in trout, salmon, cod, and narwhal, even a small whale, and kept tucking them in his wondrous little basket at his hip. But still the man on the other side of the river made his generous casts, pulling in no catch himself. They must have been at this for hours. Neither one showed fatigue. At least, not for a very long time.

It was only when the fisherman had caught absolutely nothing for about three hundred casts in a row that he began taking longer to reel the line in, and hesitated before making the next throw. But the man on the other side of the river did not stop making his perfectly precise casts. Soon, the fisherman tucked his pole into his belt and let the line sidle in the shallows. He put his hands in his pockets and watched the man on the bank cast out to him. The hook twinkled like an ornament in the heavy sun.

It wasn't long after the fisherman seemed to really notice the forest beyond the river and the sweep of wind that seemed to come from its general direction that he reached down and caught the line of the other man's fishing pole and curled his finger around the large silver hook. He paused like this as if asking, silently, if this was what he was supposed to be doing. The man in the gray hood gave a single nod, and tugged.

The fisherman kneeled down into the water, but the other did not reel. Then the fisherman took off his waders, but the other did not reel. The fisherman took off his broad-brimmed straw hat. It floated downstream. Still the stranger did not reel. Finally, the fisherman stood up and held his basket holding all his many fish before him in the water. He looked at it for a very long time with the silver hook still on his finger. The other waited. The sun was so bright on his face. Maybe he was part of the sun; he was so bright.

Finally, the fisherman pushed the basket away from himself and watched

it float after his hat and waders in the dark current. And, facing the man on the other side of the bank, he fell forward into the
water.

The gray man reeled him in as easy as though there was nothing on the line at all. When the fisherman crawled on the opposite shore, he looked different. Bigger, maybe. Fuller. Like he had adopted a new kind of strength in the undertow.

When he disappeared into the trees, I thought the gray man would follow him, since they exchanged words like old friends. Then I would wake up, or learn a big truth and realize where I was, and that things would go back to normal. But the man on the other side of the river walked farther down the shore with his pole until he was right across from me. He reached back with his bright gray arms and cast out so the silver hook landed in the very spot I'd dipped my hand.

JIANNA HEUER

SEA-GLASS

My journey has been turbulent. Through churning waves and cold dark force, the wind pulled me in all directions, landing me, not in my entirety, here at the shoreline of Rockaway Beach.

I've been riding the sea channels for years. When I was whole, a woman drank me greedily after that horrible breakup; she needed the solace only I could provide. By the end, she didn't even use her wine glass anymore; she drank straight from my neck, caressing the emerald green of my body. When she got every last drop from me, she unceremoniously threw me out.

From her recycling bin, I made the incredible journey to the dump (you know they don't really recycle anything right)? There, lying amongst the paper boxes, the rotting lettuce, the chicken bones, and the old baby clothes, I languished for what seemed like days. Then came a grizzled old man, a rummager. He went through the detritus methodically as if looking for something in particular. Now I see he is a collector of essential things, and he picked me up! He wrote a note on the back of a long receipt from Target, trotted down to Pier 39 at San Francisco Bay, and threw me into the frigid Pacific Ocean.

After a few days of pleasantly floating, I banged into a jetty. It broke me. Once nestled safely inside of me, that paper he had so lovingly placed against my curves was swept away, and as it drifted, I saw it said, "Dear Anne, I miss you..." There was more, but that was all I could see before I shattered apart.

I don't know where my other pieces have gone. I wonder what their voyages have been like. Mine has beenbeautiful, arduous, and extraordinary. I have traveled the world. I languished in the Caribbean, froze my edges off in the Arctic Ocean, and spent years hanging on the shores of Sri Lanka before being swept back into the Indian Ocean.

I fell in love on the coast of New Zealand. A gorgeous man picked me up on Hot Water Beach. He wore a wet suit that hugged all his lovely bits. He held me to the sun and gazed at all my surfaces, transfixed by my beauty. He carried me along the beach, gently rubbing me in his right hand, and I felt I was home. He came to the end of the beach and carefully laid me down on a wooden beam, an old pier sticking out of the ocean. I wished I had the words to express how I felt we belonged together. I wanted to scream, "Don't leave me!" But, of course, I can't speak, and I had to accept that we weren't meant to be. I will never forget how much I loved him, ever so briefly.

SEA-GLASS

I've been a raft to small sea creatures along the way. Snails, crustaceans, and sea horses have all used me as their Lyft to find new homes, and I've enjoyed every ride. I've landed on many other beaches just to be snatched back into the ocean, which, may I say, is much warmer than when I began my odyssey. As I lay upon this beach, I am smaller than I was years ago, about 2 inches, and a much paler green, more of a sage than an emerald. I am rubbed smooth from the years of rolling around in the ocean. I think I am ready to be picked up and taken home to be treasured by the right beachcomber. Someone who will hold me like that grieving woman once did, close to their heart.

BETH SHERMAN

YOU ARE YOUR OWN SCIENCE PROJECT

I.

The first flower bloomed along the gum line, covering my front teeth. It was followed by dozens more, curling around incisors, sprouting from the surface of my tongue – star-shaped blue petals, wispy yet compact – until eventually my lips disappeared. When I spoke, my voice sounded muffled, mysterious. Lobelia. Not my favorite. I would have preferred hydrangeas, which are showier. *You need to have them removed*, my mother said, worried what her friends would think. My father fretted about the cost – an operation would be too expensive, even after meeting the deductible. I was concerned about eating. But there were gaps between the leaves through which I could poke a straw. I drank iced tea, smoothies, matcha lattes, gazpacho, milk shakes, ice cream, candy bars and cheeseburgers pureed in the blender. I gained even more weight. When I swallowed, the lobelia would shake as though riffled by a breeze with nowhere to go. I pruned them carefully, deadheading so new blossoms would replace the old. Girls at school, who used to ignore me, invited me to parties, begged me to be their lab partner. Some of them stuffed roses between their jaws, but thorns pricked the tender pink roof of their mouths and the roses tumbled out. Boys looked at me like I was edible. *You are your own science project*, my Chemistry teacher said, not unkindly. When frost appeared one morning, coating lawns and cars, settling beneath the wings of mourning doves on telephone wires, the lobelia wilted, turning an empty shade of brown. I buried the crumbled remains in the backyard. The next summer, a single lobelia poked its face above the soil, fragile yet undaunted.

II.

One summer day, a girl was picking daisies by the side of the road. She wrapped each stem in a wet paper towel and put them in a wicker basket. The flowers were for her mother, who was dying. She didn't realize this at the time; she only knew that her mother spent all day lying in a dark room, with a damp cloth on her forehead and an army of pills on her bedside table. It was a blue-sky day, nary a cloud in the sky, hot enough to burn your tongue if you licked the pavement. The girl was thinking about water. Not the local pool, which was chlorine-fake, crowded with girls from school showing off their no-hip bodies, but the beaches she saw online, waves smashing against sugar spun sand.

As she yanked one of the daisies from the ground and threw it in the basket, its round yellow center emitted a stream of questions:

Did you do your homework?
Why won't you try to lose weight?
When you look in the mirror what do you see?
Will you miss me when I'm gone?

The girl grabbed the flower and threw it as far away as she could, which wasn't very far. She was out of breath and suddenly quite hungry. Moving cautiously, she sidled over to where she'd tossed the daisy. It was lying in the grass, leaves intact, a few of its white petals missing. Otherwise, it looked fine. She stared at it for a while, deciding, then she put it in her mouth and chewed.

III.

In Victorian times, they used to hire mutes to mourn the dead. The mutes would stand over the coffin and pelt it with violets. I learned this in my PhD program, along with a hundred other useless things most people don't know. Death enveloped the Victorians – cholera, smallpox, tuberculosis, influenza, typhus, yellow fever, scarlet fever, measles. More than one quarter of all children died before age five, meaning lots of families spent their weekends visiting tiny graves. To comfort themselves, they took dead people's haand braided it into bracelets, brooches, watches, and combs. In this way, mementos of death could be kept close to the body. Unlike flesh, human hair never decays. My mother has thin hair. When I come to visit, she opens the door with her hair curled in pink rollers. She's tried all kinds of remedies to give it more fullness – egg yolks, rosemary oil, melatonin cream, green tea soaks, something called selenium, which is supposed to keep hair follicles healthy, and mashed potatoes, one of my favorites, which I like to eat with copious amounts of grape jelly. Once, in the hospital, she let me wash it. I was telling her about the Victorians and their hair bracelets, massaging her scalp, and she took hold of my wrist, suds flying, and said *Don't you dare* and I kept easing shampoo into the limp brown strands, but what I was thinking was *you'll never know.*

PATRICK MALKA

THREE PAGES FROM MY SON'S SKETCHBOOK

The inside front cover of Jeremy's sketchbook was entirely colored black. Each parallel stroke of the sharpie clearly visible and clean, no hesitation. I could imagine how he dragged the felt tip from bottom to top, carefully covering the page. The only white was found in groups of three irregular circles made from drops of white-out, a total of six of them, eyes and the howling mouths of ghosts projected roughly from the black background of his own making. I know how my son works. Always methodical, always just a bit off. The inside front cover of the sketchbook set the tone for everything to come.

Looking through the book was not a breach of privacy. Jeremy left it on the counter before going to school with a pale green post-it that said, "feel free I'm done with this one."

We share art in this house.

I sat on the worn corduroy love seat that faced the front door and waited to hear his key hit the lock. I picked at the threads of cotton poking out of the seems of the arm rest, imagining the next thread would clear the mess and close the wound but every thread managed to carry another one through. I laughed to myself realizing the law of conservation of matter states there would be nothing left to sit on before long.

I couldn't move. There was nothing else I could imagine doing until he arrived from school. Not that there wasn't more to do. There was laundry to be folded and a bit of meal prep, not to mention the work I did from home. I had yet to finish grading three sets of lab reports and two sets of tests. Things were accumulating again. They hadn't for some time.

When Jeremy finally opened the door, he immediately laughed. I was that predictable, I guess. Good. That also meant he knew what he had done.

"Hi Dad."

"Jeremy, I need to talk about pages 11, 16 and 22."

"Alright, give me a second."

He dropped his book laden backpack next to the door and walked over to the kitchen where I could hear him wash his hands and serve himself a glass of water. When he returned to the living room, he grabbed a new sketch pad from under the coffee table and sat cross legged on the floor. He had always had an aptitude for art, but it became a compulsion after Dr. Brewer suggested art therapy could help him process more of his feelings. That was three years ago. I struggle to keep him stocked with supplies.

"Okay dad, shoot."

Page 11 was a black ink drawing of a trout. It took up the horizontal length of the page. The scales, the spots, the cartilage through each fin, the iridescence captured through meticulous cross hatching, it was all very technical in a way I had not yet seen from him. I just didn't expect the fish's head to be caved in.

"You know I went fishing with Evan and his dad, right? I didn't catch anything, and it was a slow day for them too, but Evan's dad finally catches a trout. It wasn't big but just like, bigger than I was expecting. And as quickly as he could, Evan's dad pulls out this like, flat headed hammer and bashes in the fish's head. I don't know what I was expecting, and I don't really think it was wrong. He did it fast and it was to eat it so there was a purpose. But I just got stuck on the idea of was it better for the fish that it was so quick. I don't know."

Page 16 was a pencil and charcoal drawing of a bed seen from above. The comforter on one side is smooth and undisturbed while the other side is rumpled and balled up in places. Lots of shading. Beautiful use of light and dark.

"Do you notice anything else?"

I could see that it was my comforter. The paisley pattern gave it away.

"Anything else?"

Not really no.

"My physics teacher went on a tangent a few weeks ago about what's called face pareidolia. People are kind of evolutionarily trained to see faces in things. That mountain on Mars that looks like a face and stuff like that. Look again."

I looked harder and, in the folds and pattern of the comforter on the disturbed side of the bed were several faces staring up at me. It was my side of the bed.

There were no faces on the smooth side.

Page 22 was the most provocative. As in, I believed Jeremy was trying to provoke me. I loved him for it. Simple image done in pencil of me, asleep, sitting up on the corduroy couch, a position I was finding myself in more often. Jeremy regularly woke me in the middle of the night to go sleep in bed. His intentions were good, but then I'd lay awake for hours, aware of the space I refused to occupy. In the drawing, a shadow is projected on the wall behind me. Someone else's shadow.

"There's something about you sitting in that chair dad. I don't know."

He paused, focusing on his drawing for a moment.

"I just wish I could help."

Without speaking, I pointed to the shadow in the image. He smiled again.

"No, that's no one you know."

WHEN DARKNESS COMES

1: There's No Place Like Home

Some Friday afternoon game show was a low murmur on the telly, but Tom was only giving it half an ear while he browsed a two-day old copy of the *Yorkshire Evening Post*.

Waiting was never his thing, really, especially on days like this; as ever, he was impatient to play granddad. The chores were done, the cabin prepared; there was nothing else now to occupy his mind.

When Tom finally heard the low rumble of an engine he cast aside the newspaper and grinned at the photo of Miriam on the mantelpiece: "Here they are," he growled, "let the mayhem begin!"

A few strides – he wasn't in too bad a shape for an old feller – and he was out on the patio. Down near the cabins, on the widened patch of driveway that served for guest parking, Meg's hybrid Clio was already parked up.

Raj clambered out of the passenger side and stretched, but – typical of the lad – it was Tariq who seized centre stage. Exuberant as ever, the boy's face beamed out of the near-side rear window. Tom just about heard the exited greeting: "Granddad!"

Tom chuckled and waved. The boy cracked open the door and was out of the car in a shot. An exasperated cry from his mother trailed in his wake.

Crunching gravel underfoot, Tariq raced up the path. "*Granddad!*"

The boy slammed into Tom and hugged his legs with all the enthusiasm only an eight-year-old could muster.

"Woah there, Taz, lad. Careful of an old man."

"Granddad, we saw a *shadowspire!*"

Taz's eyes shone with excitement. Tom felt the goosebumps prickle. He rallied for the boy's sake. "Oh aye, that's what they're calling 'em now, is it? Well, I suppose it fits."

"Look, Granddad!"

The boy raised his tablet so that Tom could see the screen. There it was, a narrow stripe of utter black vanishing into the sky: an uncanny streak of *wrongness*.

"Well, look at that. You passed it on the way up?"

"Yes, Granddad. It was in a field. The cows didn't like it."

"I'll bet," he muttered.

"No conspiring, you two." Meg approached, wheeling a suitcase in her wake. "Showing off his prize, is he?"

"Aye. Hello, Meg." He gave his daughter a hug. Down by the car, Raj was pulling out more luggage; he paused to wave. "Sure you brought enough?"

"Oh, Dad, give over; you're as bad as Raj. We haven't brought that much."

"So what was this shadowspire of Taz's doing?"

"Same as all the others. Nothing. Just sat there like a fault-line in reality."

Tom felt the nape of his neck prickle again. Before he found the words to respond, his granddaughter, Amy strolled over; he welcomed the distraction. Busy thumbs worked her phone, but she glanced up and brightened the mood with a dazzling smile.

"Hi, Granddad," she said, then her glance caught Taz and her features darkened to disapproval,
probably on principle.

Give the lad his due; Taz wasn't one for being sidelined so easily. "I saw the shadowspire first, Granddad," he said, glaring back at his sister. "I could have claimed it, but I had to take a picture instead."

Amy rolled her eyes. "You're the first after all the others."

"I *did* see it first, but Mummy won't let me tag it..."

"Some joker's made an app so people can track these things," Meg added. "Taz is pestering me to let him install it. They're not Pokemon, you know."

"Mummy, I know *that*!" The boy pouted. Tom chuckled, relishing the humour as an antidote to his unease.

Amy piped up: "What *are* they, Granddad?"

"Don't know, lass." Tom shrugged. "Nobody does."

Catching Meg's eye, he didn't add: *That's the trouble.*

###

Later that evening, they gathered around the telly; to Tom's mind an echo of the hearths of yesteryear.

One entertainment blended into the another, chugging out electric carbon unheeded while they caught up with small talk and goings on; background ambience, that's all it was.

Tom supped his Saltaire Blonde out of the bottle; soaked up the contended mood. Meg was on the red wine, cosied up with Raj on the couch. Earl Grey was his tipple.

"How's the cabin?" Tom asked. "Got the kids settled okay?"

Meg stifled a yawn. "Yeah, Tariq's okay on the sofa bed. I think he quite likes the adventure of slumming it. Amy's glad of a room of her own."

"So are we," Raj said, giving Meg a playful hug.

"Get off," she said, giggling. "You'll make me spill my wine!"

Raj grinned, letting go to pick up the remote; he began to flick through the channels.

"You got lucky," Tom said. "Had a last minute cancellation before you arrived. Same on the other cabin too. The folks in the cottage headed off early a day or two ago. It's these shadowspires, got people spooked, otherwise you'd all be squeezed into the spare room."

"Well, we've got Taz settled. He'd better be asleep soon, if he's not already, or Amy'll throw a fit. She's keeping an eye on him."

Tom laughed. "Oh, aye, I bet she's loving that."

"She's not quite as moody as she likes to make out."

"But don't let on her secret's out... *hey!*" Raj leaned forward, jarring Meg's elbow. She let out an exasperated cry; switching her glass from one hand to the other, she sucked spilled wine from her fingers.

Raj ignored her, intent on the screen. He pointed with the remote and turned up the volume. "Isn't that Taz's shadowspire?"

"Looks like a bunch of bloody cows to me," she replied, frowning.

"Yeah. *Look.*"

Tom leaned forward. "Something's got 'em spooked, that's for sure."

###

Somehow, the cows had broken out of their field and strayed onto the road. On any other day, the scene would have been almost comical, but not today, Tom thought; not with that bloody shadowspire lurking on the edge of shot.

They'd missed most of the pre-recorded report, but from the woman's vantage point, the cows could be seen milling around in the lanes, oblivious to the traffic backed up behind them. A couple of police cars had formed a rough and ready cordon. Several men and women were trying to herd the animals into the back of a lorry parked in the lay-by. It looked to be an awkward process.

"It appears these animals *really* don't like sharing their field," the reporter said, her tone seeming to make light of the situation.

Tom grunted at the screen. "Animals always did have more sense than folk."

"According to the police, these stragglers will be rounded up within the hour. But with more of this strange phenomenon appearing by the day, it's likely we can expect to see further disruptions like this."

The broadcast cut to the studio, where the presenter smiled calmly at his audience; just another day's routine local news, you'd think.

"It's not just these cows that are finding *The Phenomenon* unsettling," he said. "There's been a spike in reports of missing pets – cats and dogs, even feral rats – going astray. And experts are reporting an exodus of local wildlife from the vicinity of sightings, so what are they trying to tell us?"

The camera zoomed out, revealing a woman sat across from the presenter; on a screen behind him, a dark-skinned man waited patiently.

"To find out, Professor Sally Marsden from the University of Leeds has joined us in the studio, and on screen we have Doctor Anton Slattery, from Leicester University Space Centre."

"Oh, turn it off, Raj; more talking heads," Meg said.

"No, wait, let's hear what they've got to say."

Tom rolled his eyes and supped his beer. "Summat and nowt, I'll bet."

"Professor Marsden, if I could turn to you first, what do we know so far about *The Phenomenon*. Animals *really* don't like these things, do they?"

"No, it would appear not."

"So what are they trying to tell us? *The Phenomenon* appears pretty harmless. These things just stand there doing nothing, don't they?"

"They appear harmless, yes, but we would urge people not to approach these things; we can't be sure what they are doing."

"I understand that temperatures around instances of *The Phenomenon* are a degree or so cooler than the local average, so presumably they *are* doing something."

"That's right. They appear to be soaking up energy from the immediate environment. No light is reflected, no light emerges, and that's why they appear so utterly black."

"No shit," Raj muttered.

"Dr Slattery, if we can bring you in here: some scientists have suggested that *The Phenomenon* represents some kind of 'energy dead zones', fractures in the fabric of space and time itself, but I understand you're not convinced?"

"That's certainly what some in the scientific community are speculating," Slattery said. "But it is only that – speculation. The trouble is, if these filaments are 'dead zones' in local spacetime and we're just passing through them, why does each one maintain its position?"

"Perhaps you could explain for our viewers, Dr Slattery?"

"Well, the Earth is rotating and moving through space as it orbits the sun, but our parent star is also on the move – orbiting the centre of the Milky Way. Our galaxy is itself flying through the cosmos. If this *Phenomenon* represents some kind of fault in local spacetime, you would expect them to be fleeting apparitions, ghosting through the planet as we pass through them."

"I see." The presenter's tone suggested he didn't; Tom sympathised. "So what do we know about their growth?"

"We know absolutely nothing," Slattery said. "What feeds the cycle, how it's triggered, it's a mystery, and that's without even considering the mechanism. One thing we do know, when each one replicates it increases in girth and height, which seems counter-intuitive, but we've plenty of data to confirm this, at least. We're trying to identify whether these things could eventually pose some kind risk to satellites."

"Oh, how so?"

"We don't know," he said. A pause. "Maybe disrupt communications. Maybe nothing at all. We're a long way from understanding the nature of these things."

"We're not sure how deep they go, either," Marsden added. "We know from ground penetrating radar that they have a sub-surface presence in the Earth's crust."

The presenter turned in his seat. "So, why is that a concern, Professor?"

"Well, if these things are absorbing energy from the local environment, enough of them together could provoke tectonic stresses by interfering with magma flows; who knows what else? Sadly, all we can do is speculate at the moment. There are too many unknowns."

"Somebody call Doctor... no, Professor Quatermass," Tom said.

"Doctor who?"

"Quatermass. Before your time. He..." Tom stopped when he caught Raj's grin. "Yeah, okay."

"Blue Tardis to the rescue," Raj said, chuckling.

Meg nudged him with her elbow. "It's what they're not telling us, that's how I know these things aren't right."

"What do you mean, lass? Sounds dire enough to me: earthquakes and radio silence."

"Yeah, I guess, but what have they *actually* done to study these things? What's wrong with their instruments? There's something they're not telling us. Why doesn't someone pop their head in with a torch and see what's there?"

Raj laughed. "Give over, who'd want to stick their head in one of them things?"

Despite himself, Tom shivered. "Bloke down the pub told me they're portals to distant worlds. Didn't seem in a hurry to visit foreign parts himself, mind. It's just talk. Nobody knows anything; it's all make-believe to fill in the blanks."

"Maybe they *are* gates to our world; when they're ready, something's going to pop out and demand to be taken to our leader..."

Tom grunted. "God help us, then, with the clowns we've got in charge."

"Yeah, well, whatever it is," Raj added, "what can we do about it?"

"Aye." Tom nodded. "The whole world's playing Gogglebox to some eldritch cosmic occ–"

"We're on holiday is what we are," Meg said. "A family get together, and that's what we're going to do. Shadowspires, or not, we're here to relax. So enough of this morbid talk."

Tom raised his bottle. "I'll drink to that."

###

2: When Saturday Comes

To Tom's mind, this was a proper Saturday morning; blessed family time.

The kids were playing football on the lawn, leaving the 'oldsters' to take it easy on the patio.

Amy was running rings around Taz, poor lad, but she did have some nifty footwork. She also had a good five years on her brother and a habit of overplaying her advantage. *Siblings*. She took possession, nimbly dribbled the ball, kicked – and scored.

"GOAL!" Amy beamed at the adults, arms held triumphant.

"Good shot, lass!" Tom declared. Taz's mouth opened ready to howl. "Never mind, lad, you'll get one over on your sister yet."

"Two-nil. Two-nil!" Amy danced victory.

"Mummy, it's not fair! Football's a *boy's* game!"

"No such thing, Taz," Raj said, without glancing up from his phone.

Tom chuckled at the absurdities of young boys.

"Amy, go easy on Taz, okay? Give him a chance."

"Oh, Mum!" She put her hands on her hips. "It's not my fault if Tariq can't play..."

"*Amy!*"

"You've got to let me win," Taz said, smug.

"In your dreams." She did ease off; not by much, though.

"So," Tom asked, "what's the plan for today, then?"

"Oh, I don't know. Maybe we could go over to Haworth, get a taste of Bronteland, or else we could go up Ilkley-way and take a walk around the Cow and Calf Rocks. Reckon you're up to that, Dad?"

"Aye, I'll manage. I'm not that far gone. What about you, Raj?"

He was engrossed in his phone. Meg gave him a nudge. "Raj!"

"Give over," Raj said, sparking back to life. "Check this out – Chernobyl's gone."

Meg paused. "What?"

"Chernobyl." He waggled his phone. "*Telegraph* says the whole plant has been swallowed by a shadowspire."

"Bloody big place, that," Tom said, frowning. "Gone has it? Well, I don't suppose anybody's going to miss it."

"Yeah, I guess." Raj looked at his phone again. "Anyway, how can Chernobyl be *actually* gone? How can you say it's not *there* any more?"

"Well... I don't know." Tom shrugged. "What else can it be? As good as gone, then. Those shadowspires..."

"*What* is 'Chernobyl'?"

"Oh, come on Meg, you must know."

"Know what?"

"It was a bloody great nuclear reactor. Caught fire and spewed radiation over half of Europe back in '86."

"I was only four!"

"Even so," Tom said. "A whole town was evacuated, Pripyat. It's a ghost town now."

"No, it isn't. The shadowspire took the town too, apparently."

"The same one? Christ! It must be huge!"

"I guess. I don't know. Probably a cluster of the things. It's not clear from the report. It just says the town's gone too."

"Oh," Meg added. "Yeah, I remember now. I read about Pripyat. Didn't people still live there? Unofficially."

"Not any more," Raj said.

A thoughtful silence took hold, but it didn't last long before the kids interrupted. They were shouting; agitated about something.

"What is it?" Meg half turned in her chair, gasped *ohshit*...

"There's a shadowspire..."

Taz piped in: "It's in the field over there!"

Tom saw it and felt his heart sink. Beyond the grounds, across the road, two fields into the scenery, about half a mile, maybe, there it was; a thick black marker line ruled straight into the sky.

"Can we go take a look?"

Tom was surprised at the girl; less so when Tariq added: "Me too! I want to go see the shadowspire. Can we, Granddad, can we, Dad?"

"I don't think that's a good idea," Meg said.

Tom shivered. "Maybe we ought to take a look, just to be sure."

"Of what?" Raj sounded incredulous.

A shrug, Tom mumbled: "Won't know 'til we go see."

# # #

Up close, rising out of the middle of the field, the shadowspire was an even more unsettling presence; so black it wrenched at the soul.

Tom paused to catch his breath after clambering over the stile and he let the others go ahead; prickling hackles spurred a worried hand through his hair.

The scale was something else; no longer rendered a thin line by perspective, the shadowspire was as wide as a mature oak. A shadow – a real shadow – stretched across the grass; a pale imitation.

"Well now, will you look at that," he mumbled. Louder, he added: "So one of these things swallowed Chernobyl. Not much to look at, really, is it?"

Raj glanced over his shoulder. "Yeah, or else a whole lot of these things all bunched together... These things are *eating* the world."

"Don't say things like that." Meg nodded towards the kids.

"They're not daft; we can't hide them from this." Raj approached the shadowspire and peered at it, as if he might be able to see whatever was inside. "What are they waiting for, do you think? What are they hiding?"

"What do you mean, Raj?" Amy asked.

"It's an invasion!" Taz sounded far too excited at the prospect for Tom's liking.

"Don't be daft, Taz. We're not in a sci-fi movie, you know."

"Dad! I know that! But we *are* being invaded!"

Out of the mouths of babes, thought Tom, craning his neck to see the shadowspire's dizzying ascent become lost to perception. How high did this one reach?

"Let's go back," Meg said. "I don't like it."

"I know what you mean," Tom said. "Even the hairs on my bum are prickling."

Taz giggled; no one else.

"Yeah, there's nothing we can do here, I guess." Raj warily held his hand close to the Stygian surface. "Woah, feel that!"

"Raj! Don't!"

"It's okay, Amy. It's cold close up. I can really feel the difference." He shivered, as if someone had walked over his grave. Tom felt his chest chill in sympathy, as if this random stranger had hopped over his too.

The shadowspire blurred, flickered; for all the world like it was a gigantic guitar string just plucked. Tom blinked. In that instant of disconnection, the world changed with a harsh cry.

"My hand! I can't feel my hand!"

Raj staggered away from the shadowspire, right arm clutched to his chest, face scrunched up in anguish. Taz began to howl. Amy clutched at her brother; a gesture of comfort she probably needed as much as did the boy.

Meg rushed over to Raj. She took his hand in hers, gently rubbing it. "You're freezing," she said.

"Yeah." Gritted teeth. "Damn thing expanded. Swallowed my hand. Flash of cold. I mean really *cold*, it felt like my skin was burning. Now it's just numb."

The shadowspire was even thicker now. Another one had appeared towards the end of the field, just by the drystone wall, unnervingly close to the stile.

Tom tried to ignore the jitter in his knees. “We’d better get back while we still can.”

###

Back at the house, the mood was dismal. Hardly surprising, Tom knew.

He tried to make himself useful by making some tea; he plonked a mug down on the kitchen table in front of Raj.

“There you go, lad. That’ll make you feel better.”

“Thanks, Tom.” Slurred words. Raj stared at the mug, listless, while everybody else just watched and waited.

“You all right, Raj?” Tom winced at the words that almost escaped his lips. *Need a hand?*

Raj smiled weakly, as if he’d mind-read the unspoken phrase. “Yeah. Finger-licking good.”

Raj reached automatically for the mug with his limp hand. The fingers didn’t so much as even twitch, let alone grip the handle. “*Fuckssake*.”

“You’ll be right, Raj. When the feeling comes back, you’ll see.”

“Yeah. It’s just numb, that’s all.” He stared slack-faced at the cup, massaging his immobile hand in his lap.

“Let me have a look at it,” Meg said. “Dad, can you get your first aid kit?”

Tom went over and opened the cupboard. Standing on tip-toes he rummaged the top shelf, carefully removing the kit from the detritus piled on top of it.

“Here you go,” he said, placing the box on the table and opening it. “Not sure what we’ve got for hands that have had a grip of alien *nethers*, though.”

“Very funny,” Raj said, but he managed a weak chuckle.

Meg reached for Raj’s injured hand, but he pulled it away. “It’ll be okay in a while.”

“*Raj*, you’re not getting out of it that easy.” She took his hand; rubbed it in her own. She frowned. “It’s still cold, can you feel that?”

Raj shook his head and gave Tom an imploring look.

“Don’t look at me, lad. Meg’s the boss in this sort of thing; she’s the first aider in the family.”

“Yeah, enough for the office, not for dealing with unexplained cosmic phenomena. I'm going to bandage your hand lightly, Raj. Just to keep it warm, really. Don't know what else to do. Then I'll put it in a sling until you get your feeling back."

"Sure. Whatever."

Tom felt like a spare wheel watching. "I'd better do my rounds of the cabins," he said, but his heart wasn't really in it. "I'll let you get on."

"Okay, Dad. This won't take long. Do you want a cup of tea?"

"Aye. That'll do nicely."

# # #

Meg had done him one better than a cup of tea. The bottle of Speckled Hen was going to be a much-needed treat; as soon as he found the motivation to crack it open and take a swig, that is.

In truth, Tom wasn't really all that sure he was in the mood for a tipple. There was little of that earlier holiday cheer left now. Raj's lethargy was infectious. The daily routine was somehow just that much harder.

The kids had found their second wind, at least. They were out in the grounds, kicking a ball about. Tom took some comfort in the resilience of youth, but he couldn't rid himself of the sage worries of age.

Raj sat on the couch, arm trussed up, staring blankly at the telly. Reception wasn't great. The image kept breaking up, the sound warping with squawks of interference. Tom glared at the blocky screen, cursing as he flicked through the channels, looking for something more stable.

"It's the shadowspires," Raj said. "They're interfering with the signal or something."

"How do you now that, son?"

He waved his phone. "Internet was built to survive a nuclear war, didn't you know? Pity we can't take off, nuke these things from orbit. Then we could be sure."

Tom grinned. For once he got the reference; well, it was an old movie.

"Phone's patchy, though," Raj added. "Can't get hold of my folks in Leicester, but I managed to WhatsApp my brother. London's nuts, he says; lot of people leaving."

"Don't blame 'em," Tom murmured, thumbing the remote again. The next channel froze the thought. "Blow me! Didn't get this from the internet, did you?"

"Haven't checked it for a bit. What's happened now?"

"Not sure," he said, staring at the bewildering image. "Nothing good."

Tom shuffled to the couch and slumped down beside Raj. The flickering collage of images was beginning to make some kind of unreal sense; barely assisted by the reporter's attempt at calm explanation.

"What are we going to do?"

"Nowt we can do."

"All those people..." Raj broke off; little wonder. This was beyond any meaningful human sentiment. They watched together in dumbfounded silence.

Manhattan was gone; the iconic skyline erased.

The BBC reporter was struggling to convey the situation, mindlessly filling the void with words; that professional façade unmistakeably wafer thin.

They watched from the camera's vantage point, somewhere on the mainland. The sunlit sky was split vertically by the thick streak of utter darkness where once there'd been a forest of skyscrapers. A helicopter darted across the void, red light gleaming at its tail. A few glints of light shimmered from the absent city, too; evidently, this was no singular shadowspire, but a thicket of the things grown rampant.

Tom felt a pang of grief. He'd never been to New York, but he felt like he'd known that city from so many movies and shows. The loss was visceral and it stirred a lonely need for a hug; he wished Miriam – lost to cancer these three years gone – were here. But, he conceded, maybe she was better off out of it.

Raj let out a sob. Outside, the kids played on, oblivious. Tom fumbled in his pocket and retrieved his bottle opener. Small blessings.

Cut to the Whitehouse. The President had been in New York. The spokesperson urged calm. Nobody was really listening. Reporters asked furious questions, shouting over each other. The woman held up her hands, appealing for calm, then gave up. She walked off the stage, leaving uproar.

A talking head back in the BBC studio. The stock markets had plunged (although not the New York Stock Exchange, obviously). Gridlock on major transport networks; people hurrying to leave major metropolitan areas. Nobody asked where they were going to go.

Religious leaders were urging prayer. Scientists urged efforts at understanding. Most people demanded answers. None were forthcoming.

Tom finally cracked open his beer and supped it down. The taste was lost to his tongue.

###

Later that evening, they were back around the telly, this time with the kids.

Tom sat in his usual chair by the fireplace. Meg and Raj were huddled together on the couch. The kids sat cross-legged on the floor. The homeliness was hollow, though; the foolhardy mission unfolding on the screen made sure of that.

"We know what's going to happen," Raj said, dejected. He raised his bandaged hand. "They must know, too. It's a *fucking* suicide mission."

"Aye, on international telly, too."

Meg rubbed Raj's arm. "They're in the space station, that's got to offer some kind of protection, and they'll be wearing full space suits, too."

"Yeah, okay, I guess. Maybe that's something." Raj didn't seem convinced. Neither did the kids. Tom caught the glance Amy and Taz shared.

"What I don't get," Tom said "is why they don't just fly a plane through, or one of those drone thingies?"

Meg shrugged. "Guess they're worried about it falling out of the sky and landing on people."

"Oh, great," Raj said, "a space station crashing down is *so* much better."

"It's in orbit. It's not going to fall. Look, *I* don't know why, maybe they want to know how these things will affect satellites."

Tom shook his head. Even he understood it was an unlikely mission, driven by desperation. He just hoped somebody, *somewhere*, knew what they were doing.

Tom struggled to follow the bewildering collage of images, hardly helped by the intermittent squelches of blocky interference. They watched, anyway. What else were they going to do?

Even hope was holding its breath, as the crew of the International Space Station used short bursts from its thrusters to nudge the mammoth machine into an intercept orbit with the largest Manhattan shadowspire; apparently the only one to have breached the Earth's exosphere (so far).

Tom did not relish learning the new word, but the talking heads were done: little more than technobabble as prayer. Now they watched the mission in real-time. Ground-based telescopes, orbital eyes in the sky, kept track of the station's progress. Live feeds from various points on the station itself offered different angles on its approach. Chief among them was the point-of-view from the command module, curved Earth and cloudscape below – and there, on the horizon...

Tom gasped, involuntary. Framed by the station-view camera and some trick of the angle, the shadowspire wasn't so much a column, as a monolith; utter black against the hues of mother Earth; it snatched the gaze and demanded awe.

"My God, it's full of stars," he said, not so quietly as he thought.

"No, it isn't," Meg said.

"I meant... it reminds me of that film. Space Odyssey..."

"2001."

"Yeah, that's the one."

"I don't think there's any god-like aliens on the other side of this thing," Raj said.

"What's going to happen, Granddad?" Taz, wide eyed and solemn, trusting in the adults.

"Don't know, son. Let's just watch and see."

Chatter between the ISS and mission control; routine, calm. On screen, an internal shot of the station: helmeted astronauts focused on the job. Cut to a shot of mission controllers tense over their consoles; giant screens displayed live telemetry and trajectory models for all to see. Voice-over from one of the reporters; hushed comments adding little, other than to justify his pay.

Now the 'monolith' dominated the screen. Nothing but black, a faint halo of Earth-light highlighting its nothingness against the backdrop of space. The presenter fell silent, awed maybe, by sight of the shadow's maw.

"We'll be waiting for you on the far side, ISS," said the voice of mission control. "Good luck and Godspeed."

"Copy that, control. Braced for entry. Here we g–"

Radio silence. The station passed into shadow. Mission control's telemetry screens went dark. One by one the station camera feeds dropped out. Tom felt his gut clench, his lungs leaden with anticipation. Out of the corner of his eye, he saw Amy clutch Taz and hold him close.

Turgid seconds. Nobody moved, everything was frozen. Tom realised he was leaning forward; he tried to relax. The world paused.

"Come *on*," he said.

Then, just like that, it was all over. The ISS emerged from the shadowspire, reappearing on radar. A few screens in mission control kicked into life. The cheer of welcome loosened Tom's tongue, but his throat clamped down on any elation when mission control stuttered back into silence. No comms. No telemetry. Dead screens.

The station was reacquired on camera. Drastically decelerated, the ISS tumbled in a lazy, decaying orbit; systems down, no power. Even so, desperate ground control crew tried frantically to raise the astronauts. Belatedly, the transmission cut to studio presenters, rallying as best they might.

It took a while for it all to sink in. Then Raj grumbled: "So much for space suits."

# # #

3: Sunday Brings No Rest for the Afflicted

There were even more of the things out there this morning; through the kitchen window Tom's once heartening view of the Yorkshire countryside was riddled with black lines.

Tom tried to ignore the disconcerting sight, but it was right there on the periphery of his vision, nagging for attention. Even so, he attempted to lose himself in the dish washing. They'd let it build up; he wasn't normally so slack with the chores.

The crackly radio was proving no diversion, but the alternative was brooding silence. Meg, Raj and the kids were in their cabin; maybe they were still asleep. He'd always been an early riser. Semi-retirement hadn't changed that. Listening to the news, he felt like crawling back to bed and pulling the covers over his head. One way or another, it was all shadowspires.

Tom wasn't really listening, just absorbing the information through some kind of mental osmosis. The ISS had crashed into atmosphere and broken up over the Atlantic Ocean; that had pricked his ears up. The fiery debris had burned up before it could reach Europe, not that it mattered too much.

More cities had effectively vanished overnight. The loss of life was unimaginable. The lack of real *knowing* only made it worse. And here he was, wiping suds off a dinner plate, as if normality remained an option.

It had all happened so fast, the shift from curiosity to abject fear. In the wake of Pripyat, Manhattan, and now so many more, where was the sturdy redoubt beyond *The Phenomenon's* reach?

Refugees were jamming roads the world over as bewildered people sought to flee population centres, fearful they might go the same way as a growing list of towns and cities. The centre of Leeds was gone too, riddled with shadowspires, far too close for comfort.

Bradford had set up centres for displaced people, even though this mysterious blight was nibbling away its urban fabric too; other nearby towns were following suite. The countryside was no better; he saw that plain enough through his window.

Drying his hands, Tom could only shake his head. "What the hell can I do about it, anyway?"

The flash of anger he felt was a surprise.

###

By the time he'd finished his chores, the kids were outside kicking a ball about again.

Tom scrunched down the gravel path and left them to their game. The sounds of their play gladdened his old heart, but not enough to lift his sombre mood: not with all those shadowspires encroaching on his little patch of world.

He found Meg outside the cabin, pacing beneath the old beech tree. She looked how he felt; shoulders hunched, face a frown. She had her phone clamped to her ear, free hand clenched at her chest.

She looked up as Tom approached, returned his greeting with a taut little wave. Then she removed the phone from her ear and tapped the screen. "*Sugar!*"

"Who you trying to get hold of?"

"*Everybody*," she barked, exasperated. Then she swore properly and some of the tension went out of her shoulders. "I figured I ought to try and get hold of Amy's father. The dead-beat isn't answering, as usual, just his voicemail. Tried to get some medical advice for Raj, too. Can't get through. Lines are busy or the connection just drops out."

"It's them shadowspires," he said. "They're causing havoc from what I heard on the radio. There's power out in some places. Surprised we've got any kind of reception at all."

Meg thrust her phone into a pocket. "Can't even get onto *bloody* Facebook to leave a message for Raj's brother!"

"Is he up? How's he doing?"

"He's not getting any better. I've told Taz and Amy it's just a bad cold. I don't know... Dad, *I'm really worried...*"

###

Tom tucked a blanket under Raj's chin and felt his forehead. He looked like he was burning up; he felt cold and clammy.

"I've got to ring Mum," he said through the feverish shivers, forgetting he'd tried plenty of times before in the days gone.

A glance at Meg; she shook her head. Whether that meant she'd tried and couldn't get through or else Raj's mum was lost in some shadowspire, he didn't know. He tried to remember if Leicester was on the list of lost settlements, but his mind remained blank.

"Later, lad," he said, moving aside to give Meg room. "You try to rest."

Sick as he was, Raj wasn't keen on playing patient. Meg sat beside him and gently removed his arm from beneath the blanket, but when she began to fiddle with his dressing, he flinched and tried to fend her off.

"I'm okay," he rasped. "Just let me alone."

"Come on, Raj, lad," Tom said. "We can all see you're not right."

"Dad's right, Raj. Now stop fussing and let me look at your hand."

Raj gestured in defeat. Meg took hold of his hand and began to unwrap the bandage. After a while she paused. Her face went pale and she blanched.

"Oh, Raj..."

Tom stepped forward to get a better view and instantly regretted it. The skin on Raj's hand was discoloured, almost black at the fingertips. There was a faint scent of spoiled meat.

"We need to get you to A&E," Meg said.

Raj pulled his arm out of her grip. "I'm all right. I'll be fine."

"Raj! *Look* at it!" Meg's voice cracked. "We're going, whether you like it or not."

###

Amy held Tariq's hand while Meg fussed over Raj and guided him to the car. Tom stood by with the kids, supposedly a reassuring presence, but he wasn't feeling too sure of himself right now.

"Will Dad be okay?" the boy asked, bringing Tom out of his reverie.

"He'll be all right, Taz. The doctors will sort him out. He'll be back right as rain."

"That's what Mum said about Nana," Amy said. "But she died anyway."

Taz turned and hugged his sister; he'd never really had the chance to know his grandmother, so he wasn't anywhere near so worried.

"You kids be good, okay?" Raj called from the car. He looked haggard and tired, all pretence abandoned.

"We won't be long. Don't worry," Meg called. She climbed into the driver's side and slammed the door.

Tom watched the car pull away and he put his arms around the kids. His eyes strayed to the distant clutter of darkness that marked what had once been the city of Leeds. "It'll be fine," he said.

###

The day wore on. No word from Meg; Tom tried not to fret.

Keeping the kids occupied was easier said than done; boredom wasn't the problem, more a listless unease that was hard to shake.

DVDs just gave them something to stare at. The same might be said for their personal screens; whatever was left out there in the digital world wasn't up to much, going by their mutters of frustration.

Tom found little solace in his own screen, between their stock of family movies reception was worse than ever. The radio wasn't much better. The news channels kept a steady flow of doom and gloom, so not much change there.

Oh, but the conspiracy theorists were having a field day. Most were the usual run of alien interference or deities run amok. With places cooling in the vicinity of the spires, some were even saying it was a secret geo-engineering project; an attempt to address global warming gone wrong.

Back in the real world, a shadowspire had swallowed Parliament, not so funny now it had *actually* happened. The Beeb's Broadcasting House was likewise gone; its MediaCity base in Salford had stepped in to provide an emergency national base, but with neighbouring Manchester speckled with shadowspires it was anybody's guess for how long.

In world news, earthquakes had hit California. There were volcanic eruptions in Indonesia and Iceland. Scientists were in a sweat over the weakening of the Earth's magnetic field. The economies of the world were in freefall. Governments were rattling sabres over long-standing bones of contention; well, he supposed it was easier than fathoming *The Phenomenon's* implacable appetite.

Eventually Tom gave up; it was all too much. He switched off the telly and tried to rouse the kids from their lethargy.

"Come on, you two," he said, forcing some enthusiasm into his manner. "Why not have a kick around outside? Make the most of the weather..."

Taz looked up. "Is Dad okay?"

"Don't know, lad. No news is good news."

"Where are they? Why hasn't Mum called? At least *texted*. Why doesn't she answer her phone?"

"She will, lass. When she can. It can get right busy up at A&E. It's only been a few hours. They could be there all night, you know."

"So why isn't she answering; why hasn't she *called?*"

###

Tom knew he must be a pathetic sight, but he had to hold it together for the kids' sake.

A call of nature was the only way Tom knew to hide away while he released some of the grief. So, here he was, sat on the bog: an old man with his pants down around his ankles, weeping into his palms.

He removed his hands from his face and glanced at his mobile phone placed on the edge of the bath; nothing fancy, just a basic handset. Without thinking, he snatched it up and thumbed Meg's speed dial again. The phone went through the motions of trying to connect. The attempt ended with an abrupt message: unobtainable. Not even voicemail operating.

Face facts; they were gone. Meg and Raj. What was he going to tell the kids?

No, there had to be hope. The shadowspires were playing havoc with systems. Too much infrastructure consumed. His little girl was still out there, *somewhere*. What would Miriam say, seeing him like this? Well, she'd never seen him, *before*, when the cancer was pulling them apart; he'd made sure of it, so he could present as outwardly strong. But she'd never been a fool; she probably knew. That was his Miriam.

Tom sniffed. Tore off a strip of toiler paper and wiped his eyes. Then he began to fumble his clothes back into place; call of nature unheeded.

Taz and Amy needed their tea. No, they needed their mum and dad, at least the illusion for a little while longer. Magic only their granddad could muster; he pulled up his pants – and himself together – ready to deliver.

###

Tom went straight to the phone and dialled.

It was an old rotary thing, modified to work on a modern net – something he'd got just to baffle the kids, really – but Amy had long-since dismissed its retro charm. She regarded him now with a sceptical scowl; clearly she didn't believe it worked, but when he spoke into the mouthpiece he was gratified to see the girl's jaw drop.

"Meg? *Meg!* Can you hear me, you're crackling up – it's your dad."

He paused to listen; gave Amy a quick smile.

"You've tried ringing? Yeah, us too. Guess the network's feeling the strain. What's that you say?"

Tom frowned, concentrating.

"Say that again. Amy wants to know, how's Raj?"

Another pause. Amy fidgeted.

"Tests you say? Meg? Meg, you're breaking up. What's that? Yes, I'll tell her. Okay, yes... bye. Oh, Meg... ah, she's gone."

He turned to Amy. "Your mum is fine, she says hello. They want to do some tests on Raj so they'll be a while yet."

Amy folded her arms and glowered. "I wanted to speak to Mum!"

"I know, lass. I'm sorry. The line was real bad, you heard, right? I think she was being called by the docs. She had to go."

"S'pose." Amy sighed. She turned and shuffled back into the living room.

Tom didn't quite let the mask slip, but he felt his body sag as he put the dead handset back on the cradle. Amy wasn't the only one clinging to *hope*.

# # #

4: In Days Gone By

Monday came and went. Still no word from Meg; Tom wasn't expecting any.

The kids didn't talk about it; numb inevitability. Tom didn't know if that was a good thing, but he couldn't find the words to broach the subject. He wondered if they'd seen through his ruse with the phone.

They grieved, each their own way; throwing themselves into routine, pretending the absence was only temporary. Tom and the kids stared at screens – the telly, tablets, phones, even his old PC – and watched helpless as the world was switched off piece by piece.

Conversation became basic; life was reduced to a skeletal routine – food, toilet, sleep (fitful at best). The kids did what they could, helping with the cabins, which was much, though the point of it now was elusive; something to do, Tom figured. Amy's tone had softened towards her brother, but who could say how long the armistice would last once – *if* – life returned to normal.

Kids were often a misrule unto themselves, Tom remembered. There was a blessing in that, somewhere.

###

They lost power in the night. Tom was rattling around in the kitchen, making the kids something to eat when the lights dropped out.

Amy yelled: "Granddad!"

"It's okay, probably just a fuse." But that didn't explain why what remained of the distant streetlamps through the kitchen window had all gone dark too.

He stumbled, felt for the drawer, then fumbled for the torch. A cone of vision rewarded his efforts and he shuffled towards the fuse box by the kitchen door. A frown as he unlatched the cover and shone the light at the meter.

"Well, bugger it," he muttered, but he wasn't really surprised. The circuit breakers on the main board were all in the on position. So much for that.

"Power's out," he shouted.

"We know, Granddad," Taz called back. "Put the lights back on!"

"Can't, son. Problem's out there with the grid somewhere."

Grunting back to his feet, he rubbed his stubbled chin; now, where were they?

He remembered and went to one of the cupboards. A quick rummage and he pulled out a couple of
battery powered lanterns. Should last the night, he mused.

"Here, isn't this cosy," he said, positioning the lanterns around the front room. "What are your gadgets telling us?"

"No wifi, Granddad!" Taz said, sulky voiced.

Amy tapped at her phone. "I've got some data left." She stared at the screen, lips moving soundlessly "It's slow. Got something. Shadowspires have taken out a power station and some other stuff. They're trying to work out a fix."

"Good luck with that one," Tom said softly. Louder: "Well, that explains why the horizon's gone dark. Well, what's left of it. Don't you kids worry, we can survive a power cut."

"But what about my phone, Granddad? I'll need to charge it soon!"

"Don't fret, lass. We'll make do."

"Granddad! This is *serious*, how will we know what's going on?"

"What if Mum tries to call?" Taz said, his voice croaking on the edge of tears.

###

5: In the Wide Beyond

Morning brought no respite, anything but.

Tom stepped out to stand on the patio and let his eyes slowly take in the view. There were so many shadowspires out there now they were soaking up enough daylight to darken the scenery. If he didn't know better, he'd swear it was dusk.

Most were still some way off, forests of the things. But some of the blighted scenery was too close to home. A cluster brooded in the fields beyond his property. Another shadowed a lamppost on the road itself. Worse, a shadowspire rose out of cabin number two, sealing off the door by the look of it. Nobody was getting in that way. A blessing it wasn't occupied.

Sudden movement on the edge of his vision turned his head; the shadowspire in the road flickered. Blinking away the discomfort, when Tom opened his eyes he saw the lamppost was gone; absorbed inside the dark column, now visibly thicker. Another one had appeared in the grounds, out by the boundary with the road. A fresh cluster blighted the fields, closer still to his shrinking domain.

Tom rubbed his face and groaned. They were fast running out of options. No power. A short supply of spare batteries. Plenty of water, but food running low. No word on what was out there, in the wide world. But his old eyes told him what was right here on his doorstep. The darkness was closing in.

"Sitting tight is getting us nowhere," he huffed, stepping back inside.

The kids eyed him quizzically. Sat at the kitchen table, a hasty breakfast of jam and bread barely touched, they looked worn out, poor things. Tom felt little better. He sighed; giving vent to a weariness that went beyond his years.

"We can either wait here for these shadowspires to swallow us up, or we can go see if we can find somewhere they can't reach us. See if we can't find your mum and Raj along the way, eh?"

Amy looked solemn. “Is it safe?”

No lies, not now. “Don’t know, lass. Maybe no-where’s safe,” he nodded towards the window, “but we’re sure enough getting boxed in here.”

“I want to find Mum and Dad!”

Tom turned his gaze to the boy and nodded. “Aye, lad, let’s go find ‘em.”

# # #

The decision to make a move had taken years off his shoulders, going by the way he took the stairs; even so he was huffing and puffing by the time he reached the landing.

Amy and Taz were arguing over what to take; voices a bickering background as he stomped towards the master bedroom. Sure, he’d told the kids to pack only what they absolutely needed, but an old man couldn’t be grudged a memento of the life he once had. In any case, he wasn’t leaving Miriam behind.

Tom scurried over to the bedside cabinet, scooped up the framed photograph of his late wife, the one with Meg and the grandkids all together. She looked pale and tired in it, a headscarf covering her baldness, but the smile held all the life she needed as she beamed happily at the camera.

Next, he stooped beside the dresser and reached for the lower drawer; a photo album – just one – for old time’s sake. The drawer was stuck. He grunted, straining until it opened. A sudden sense of chill air raised his hackles.

The room grew noticeably darker. The kids had gone quiet. Tom felt the emptiness of the house as a cold lump in his gut. There were no tears, not yet, just resignation. He called out anyway.

“Amy, Tariq?”

Silence.

“Come on,” he shouted, his voice cracking. “Don’t play silly buggers with an old man!”

# # #

Beyond the bedroom window, there was little to see.

The view wasn’t entirely pitch black; some light managed to percolate downwards from the lost sky, but a cluster of shadowspires abutted the house, blocking sight of all but a strip or two of the outside world.

Tom’s vision swam; he reached for the windowsill to steady himself. Fear was pointless, but it tickled his ribs all the same. A clump of it weighed down his stomach. He wiped his eyes and glanced towards the door. There was no getting out that way; a shadow stood sentinel on the landing.

"Granddad!" Now he was hearing things. Grief was funny in its ways. He clutched the photoframe and swallowed a sob. The voice again. It sounded muffled, distant... from outside the house.

He cracked the window open, pushed it wide as he dared. A flush of cold through the handle as the frame's exterior met a shadowspire's surface; he quickly let go.

"Granddad!"

The voice was real. Tom's breath caught; he coughed and managed to get his tongue around a reply.

"Taz! Tariq, up here, lad!"

The boy's face peered up between a gap in the gloom. "Granddad, you're alive!"

"That I am, Taz. Can't be rid o' me that easy." Despite the circumstances, a smile seized his face. "What about your sister, where's Amy?"

"I'm here, Granddad."

Well, that was two of his prayers answered. Shame about the third, but that would be pushing his luck.

Tom tried to peer through the gaps between the spires. Aside from the partial view of Taz he couldn't see Amy, but he'd settle for the sound of her voice.

"What happened?" His voice almost failed. "I thought they got you."

"We went to the cabin. Taz wanted some of his things."

"We can't get back in, Granddad. The shadowspires are blocking the doors. They're everywhere."

"I know, son. They're in here, too. I'm blocked in."

"What are we going to do, Granddad?"

"You've got to look after Taz, Amy; get him out of here."

Taz bawled. "No, Granddad!"

"We can't leave you." Amy wasn't so far off tears herself. "You have to get out of the house!"

"I can't lass. Not unless I could knock through the walls, and this old house is built solid. The shadowspires have got me blocked in good."

"There must be something we can do."

"No, Amy. You have to go."

"NO!"

"There's nowt you can do for me." Harsh voice, no regret; the kids had to understand. "But you can get Taz somewhere safe."

"*Where?*"

"Anywhere, lass. Do it for me. Just go."

# # #

With a sigh, Tom closed the curtains. It was a futile gesture, but there was a homely defiance that reminded him of better days. Shut out the weather, that was it, cosier this way.

The kids were gone. He ought to feel relieved, he knew, but it was a bad old world out there, now. Well, there was nothing he could do about it. With luck they'd find somewhere safe. If there was such a place. Maybe they really would find Meg and Raj. He hoped so.

Tom wasn't ready to face the end; he had to brace for it all the same. Miriam must have felt much the same, he guessed.

The darkness at the door was waiting for him. Tom turned to regard it. The lantern he'd left on top of the dresser spilled some of its light out onto the landing. The glow dispersed the mundane dark to reveal the shadowspire's lurking presence. Most of it was hidden behind the bedroom wall; what remained to sight gave every impression of peering into the room, as if waiting for an invitation to enter.

Tom wondered – just a crazy thought, really – was the shadowspire actually *watching* him? He shivered, not from the chill air. "Energy dead zone, my arse."

The shadowspire flickered as if in response; not any kind of answer Tom desired. When his eyes adjusted, he saw that the thing was in the room now, protruding through the wall.

Tom shuffled backwards to the careworn armchair in the corner of the room furthest away. Forlorn, he hugged Miriam's photo to his chest and let the weight of fate pull him down into the chair.

There, he sat and watched; waiting for the darkness to take him.

BIOGRAPHIES

RUE DION is a 21-year-old female based in South Africa, who is a passionate poet with a big heart, one that aches for all people. She aspires to write professionally and be the voice for those who feel but cannot put what is in their hearts and minds into words. She can be found and read on Tumblr @thechroniclesoforphic or found on Instagram @its.rue_

ERAN FARROW is a forty-year-old multiple sclerosis survivor and an Oklahoma native set on changing the world through words and questions.
Twitter @efarrow1973

LAURA SUTHERLAND is an artist and farmer in her early twenties from the Great Lakes region. She often grapples with the idea of home and tries to answer the question: what does the earth ask of us? In addition to poetry, Laura writes music, singing while playing the piano or ukulele, and painting in watercolor. Her work can most easily be found on Instagram and Tumblr @lauramaywrite

RAINA GAVIN is a poet living in Montana. You can find her browsing a thrift store, chasing after her three cats, snuggling her blind French bulldog and her three-legged Italian greyhound, or pacing at three am, powered only by millennial ennui. Oh, or Tumblr @cemetery-fox

THOMAS DIMASSIMO. Thomas DiMassimo is an Italian-American writer from Atlanta, GA. In addition to his late night Tumblr musings, Thomas also works as a screen and television writer. He does not recommend you ever order anything called 'disco fries.'

DAMON HUBBS writes poems about Thulsa Doom, Italo disco & girls who cry at airports. He's the author of two chapbooks (most recently *Coin Doors & Empires,* from Alien Buddha Press). His work has appeared in *Lothlorien Poetry Journal, Apocalypse Confidential, Dreich, Acropolis Journal, Cutbow Quarterly,* & elsewhere. Twitter @damon_hubbs

ANDI LEIGH is a Filipino-American poet, novelist, and short story writer from Western Massachusetts. They began writing at a young age and enjoy writing poetry about death, loss, love, and nature. Their short stories center around themes of horror and the supernatural. Social media: @andileighwrites (Instagram, Threads, Tumblr)

JAY GOLDIN works in academia and journalism. He has published poetry, fiction, film essays, book reviews, and photographs.

NEIL G is a poet, novelist and essayist. He loves the era of the romantic poets and their passion for verse and the natural world. He also walks the traditional corridors of ghostly tales and gothic horror. He reads the Runes, having studied the Teutonic Traditions. He can be found @Banquozghost on Platform X formerly known as Twitter.

JUNAID AHMED AHANGAR works as a doctor in a tertiary care institute in Srinagar, Kashmir. He graduated from Dhaka, Bangladesh and completed his MD in Medicine from Srinagar, Kashmir. He also has an MA in English Literature from India and is currently in the second year of MA in Philosophy. He devotes his time between his profession and passions which over the last few years has seen a conscious departure towards writing poetry and prose. He is also a singer-songwriter and occasional guitarist with other interests apart from literary pursuits like music, film-making, podcasting and theology.

BRANDON T BENNETT is a Northern English poet from Manchester, UK. A father of two, his debut pamphlet will be published by Death of Workers Whilst Building Skyscrapers in early 2024. Other examples of his work can be found in Broken Sleep Books, Live Canon, and BRAG Writers Literary Magazine. X: @ BrandonThomasB

SHAYNE JOHNSON was raised in Michigan and currently resides in Southern California. After college, he pursued a career in Logistics which opened doors to a world of travel. Upon spending a couple of years throughout China, his passions of pursuit include, but aren't limited to: long-distance backpacking, camping, hunting, diving and cherishing his time with friends and family.

YASH SEYEDBAGHERI is a graduate of Colorado State University's MFA fiction program. His stories, *Soon, How To Be A Good Episcopalian, Tales From A Communion Line,* and *Community Time,* have been nominated for Pushcarts. Yash's work has been published in *SmokeLong Quarterly, The Journal of Compressed Creative Arts, Write City Magazine,* and *Ariel Chart,* among others.

PETER BILES is a fiction writer and essayist. He graduated from Wheaton College (IL) and received a Master of Fine Arts in creative writing from Seattle Pacific University. He lives in Oklahoma.

JIANNA HEUER is a psychotherapist in private practice in New York City. She writes creative nonfiction and has been published in *Across The Margin, Hot Pot Magazine,* and *Underscore Magazine.* Her flash nonfiction has appeared in two books, *Fast Funny Women* and *Fast Fierce Women.*

BETH SHERMAN has an MFA in creative writing from Queens College, where she teaches in the English department. Her stories have been published in *Portland Review, Black Fox Literary Magazine, Blue Mountain Review, Tangled Locks Journal, 100 Word Story, Fictive Dream, Flash Boulevard, Sou'wester* and elsewhere. She is also a Pushcart Prize, Best Small Fictions, and a multiple Best of the Net nominee. She can be reached at @bsherm36

WORM CARNEY is a part-time writer from a small town on the east coast of Ireland. Upon mourning her first loss, Worm discovered a deep-rooted appreciation for life, love and even death—all three of which influence her works. She is on Tumblr @imfullofworms

TESSA YOUNG is a lover of the natural world and a writer of poetry and prose. She writes as a way to contemplate the world around us while also trying to dive deep into the self as a way to grow through life with an appreciation for the little things. She can be found on her website tessdeanne.com or on Tumblr @ accessyoursoul

DONOVAN BALDWIN is a retired U.S. Army, seventy-eight-year-old caregiver. He began writing teenage angst poems in the 1960's until encouraged to open up by a lady in Germany in 1968, who read one of his poems on a bar napkin and praised his work. He writes poems on many subjects, but especially romance, with dips into eroticism. His poetry was published in various magazines in the 80's, and his poems have been published and reviewed in Ponder 2021 and Ponder 2022, including his poem, Naked Outside Of Eden. He can be found and his poetry can be read on X (Twitter), as @donovanbaldwin.

PATRICK MALKA (he/him) is a high school science teacher from Montreal, Quebec, where he lives with his partner and two kids. His flash fiction can be found in Five South's *The Weekly, Broken Antler Magazine, Maudlin House, Nocturne Magazine,* and *Sky Island Journal* among others. He can be found online on Twitter @PatrickMalka and patrickmalkawriter.ca.

MARK CANTRELL is a UK-based writer and journalist with two novels under his belt so far. He has recently returned to work after spending three years caring for an elderly parent with dementia. It was quite the experience, he says. Currently, he's working on his third novel. You can find him on Twitter (X, if you must) @Man0Words

www.ingramcontent.com/pod-product-compliance
Lightning Source LLC
LaVergne TN
LVHW070143110826
845147LV00002B/315

* 9 7 9 8 9 9 9 3 9 9 1 7 5 *